DYLAN'S SECRET . . .

Courtney waited while Dylan got comfortable on the hospital bed. She could see, from the way he was still holding his wrist, that he was in pain.

''I've never broken anything,'' Courtney said. ''It looks like it really hurts, huh?''

''Yeah,'' Dylan said. ''It does.'' Then, to her surprise, he reached out his injured hand and took her hand in his.

''Courtney . . . could you hold my hand? Just for a minute,'' he said.

Courtney's heart raced as he closed his fingers tightly around hers. Could this really be happening? Was he really trying to tell her he liked her?

Read all the **FIFTEEN** books:

Dylan's Secret

Editorial services by Parachute Press, Inc.

Cover photo by Mark Malabrigo

FIFTEEN ™

Dylan's Secret

By Megan Stine

PUBLISHERS · GROSSET & DUNLAP · NEW YORK
in association with Nickelodeon Books™

CHAPTER 1

DYLAN SAT IN his last period English class and tried to look like he was listening.

I should have cut class, he thought to himself. He mindlessly drew circles on a blank piece of notebook paper as he stared at the clock. Mondays were the worst. Waiting for the bell to ring was torture. Finally at 3:00, the electronic beep signaled that school was over.

I'm outta here, Dylan thought. He headed straight for the door and slipped out of class before anyone could stop him. Today he had big plans.

"Hi, Dylan." Two eighth-grade girls smiled at him as he passed them in the hall. Dylan nodded. His light brown hair fell forward and he gave the girls a little smile. Ever since his band had played at the Avalon, Dylan had been sort of a celebrity at school. It made him feel pretty good.

When he reached his locker, he stuffed his books inside and grabbed his black leather jacket. He could hardly wait to get out of the building, away from school.

"Hey, Dylan?"

Dylan turned around and saw Billy standing behind him. Billy was 14, only a year younger than Dylan, but he seemed a lot younger. His silky-smooth blond hair made him look like a choirboy compared to Dylan, and he was just short enough and gawky enough to look like someone's kid brother. In fact, he was someone's younger brother—Courtney's, a girl in Dylan's class. But Dylan treated Billy like a brother of his own.

"Hi, Billy. What's up?"

"I just wanted to ask you a question," Billy said.

Dylan eyed the clock at the end of the hallway. "I'm in kind of a hurry," Dylan said. "But okay. What's your question?"

"Well, this other guy and I were talking about Sid Franks—you know, the lead guitarist for Death Station? And he said Sid is left-handed. But I said, no way. Just look at his music video and you can see—he plays the guitar like everyone else. Right-handed. So I told him we should ask you because you know practically everything about guitar."

Dylan smiled and checked the clock again. "I hate to tell you this," Dylan said, "but the guy is right. Sid Franks is left-handed. But he plays like a rightie."

"Really?"

"Yeah," said Dylan. "I heard him interviewed once, and he said that when he was a kid he was too poor to have his own guitar; he had to use his brother's old one. He couldn't afford to have it restrung. So he just learned to play right-handed."

"Wow! I knew you'd know," Billy said admiringly.

"It's just basic," Dylan said.

"So can we practice today?" Billy asked.

Dylan shook his head and started walking down the hall. "Not today. Got other plans."

"Oh," Billy said, looking totally rejected.

Dylan took one look at the expression on

Billy's face and caved in. "You want to come along?" he asked.

"Sure! Where're we going?"

"The 84 raceway. A friend of mine has been teaching me how to ride his bike."

Billy laughed. "Didn't you learn how to ride a bike when you were six?"

"Not a *bicycle*," Dylan said with a hint of contempt. "A motorcycle. A big huge machine."

"Oh, cool! I mean, leave it to you to be tearing up the streets before you even get your license!" Billy said admiringly.

"Yeah."

Dylan's heart pounded an extra beat as he thought about the first time he had straddled the huge motorcycle and felt its weight almost knocking him down. He had struggled to hold it up, gripping the handlebars with all his strength, trying not to let his effort show. The bike wasn't quite what you'd call a "hog," but considering Dylan's slight build, it was hard enough to control. But, riding a motorcycle was a kind of heart-stopping thrill. Maybe the fact that Dylan was too young to ride it legally had something to do with it.

"Whose bike is it, anyway?" Billy asked.

"A guy I know's," Dylan said. "Neil Durrant."

Billy looked a little confused. "Is he a senior?"

"No," Dylan laughed again. "He graduated. A few years ago, I think. Anyway, he's not in school."

"Cool!" Billy said with twice as much enthusiasm.

Dylan had been so focused on the idea of riding Neil's motorcycle that he was surprised to find they'd walked the whole length of the school and had reached the soccer field.

"Hi, Dylan," a girl said, crossing in front of him. It was Ashley, one of the girls Dylan knew but didn't exactly hang out with, mainly because she had been going with Matt, the super-jock. Ashley was the complete opposite of Dylan— friendly, outgoing, and a good student. Dylan was private, independent, rebellious, and more into his music than anything else. "Coming to the soccer game?" Ashley asked.

"I've got other plans," Dylan said, smiling a bit to let her know that he didn't mind being asked.

"Well, maybe next time," Ashley said.

"Yeah," Dylan said. "Next time."

But in his heart he knew that the only way he'd ever show up at a game was if they asked his band to play at the pep rally beforehand.

"Maybe, sometime, your band could play at one of the pep rallies," Ashley said.

"That's weird!" Dylan said, smiling at her.

"Why?" Ashley asked.

"You must be reading my mind!"

The "84 raceway" was really just a closed section of expressway, about a mile from school, on Route 84. But even though there were wooden barricades across the off-ramps, everyone used the road anyway. On Saturday afternoons, parents took their kids there to teach them how to drive. And at night, teenagers used it as a drag strip to race cars and motorcycles. That's why it was called the "84 raceway." Dylan had even seen middle-aged rich guys from the city there, racing their Porsches up to 150 miles per hour.

But this afternoon, as Dylan and Billy arrived, the road looked deserted except for a strip of red cloth that was draped like a streamer on the wooden barricade.

"Come on. They're here," Dylan told Billy, who was a few steps behind him. Billy had to run to catch up with him. The road looked flat, but it actually sloped uphill slightly, and then down, so that you couldn't see what was over the crest of the hill until you got there. Billy followed, and when they reached the top, they saw five guys standing in the hollow, just out of sight.

"Hey—I thought you said you were meeting some guy named Neil. I mean, this looks like a whole motorcycle gang," Billy said uncertainly.

"Looks like a race to me. Let's go," Dylan said, moving toward the group. But then Dylan frowned. I wonder if Neil will let me ride with all these guys around, he thought to himself.

As they got closer, Dylan checked out the other four guys. They were all about Neil's age, in their 20's maybe. One guy was wearing a bright yellow windbreaker and black shorts that matched the hot yellow and black paint on his bike. With his summer tan and sun-streaked hair, he looked more like a surfer than a biker. The other guys looked like serious motorheads, though. Big mean-looking bikes and black leather jackets to match. They had obviously been working on their motorcycles, because there was a pile of tools spread out on a greasy towel on the ground.

Dylan gave Billy a quick sideways look that said, "Didn't I tell you this would be great?"

"Dylan, my man!" Neil said, giving Dylan a cool low-five slap. Neil's shoulder-length blond hair was tied in a ponytail, and he had on a heavy metal t-shirt that barely reached the waistband of his torn jeans.

"Who's this? Your junior fan club?" one of the leather-jacketed guys said to Neil, gesturing to Dylan.

"Kid I'm grooming to be the next Evel Knievel," Neil joked. "And his sidekick. Anyway, are you guys going to bang around with these cylinders all day? Or are you ready for a race?"

No one answered Neil. They all simply climbed on their bikes and pumped the kick-starters. Neil dragged the towel of tools off to the side of the road.

"Hey, Neil—am I going to get a chance to ride?" Dylan asked.

"Yeah, probably, man. After this race goes down. You don't want to mess with these guys in a race."

"Yes, he does!" Billy suddenly spoke up from behind. "You want to race, don't you Dylan?"

"Uh, yeah—sure," Dylan said. But inside, he

wasn't exactly sure. Race? Right now? He'd barely learned to control the huge machine, and these guys looked *serious*.

"Come on," Billy whined. "What are you waiting for, Dylan? I mean, this is awesome! You'll totally whip these guys!"

"Well?" Neil said, looking at Dylan for some kind of answer. "Do you think you can handle it?"

"Of course he can handle it!" Billy said.

Dylan tried to ignore Billy. "I can handle it," Dylan said to Neil. "But what if I total your bike?"

The guy with the yellow windbreaker was close enough to overhear Dylan's words. "What if he falls and skins his wittle knees?" he said, taunting Dylan in a baby voice.

"Come on, Dylan!" Billy sounded desperate for Dylan to come through. "You aren't going to let these guys scare you, are you?"

"No way," Dylan snapped.

"Hey, you'll be fine, man," Neil said, kick-starting his bike. "I mean, I wouldn't let you even *touch* my bike if I thought you'd wreck it. And anyway, you're a natural. I told these guys—I never saw anyone learn to ride so fast as you."

"Yeah," Dylan said, uncertainly. But it was true. Last week, Dylan had whipped through the gears on Neil's bike like they were nothing. It was a kick and a half.

"Just remember what I told you about leaning with the bike on the curves. Especially when you get to the off-ramp."

"Yeah—you'd better get off and *walk* his bike on the off-ramp," the guy in the windbreaker said, giving Dylan a mean laugh.

Dylan couldn't believe this was happening— and it was happening too fast. Sure—he was a quick learner. But something told him that he was crazy to race right now. Especially since this was only the third time he'd ever ridden a bike in his life! For half a second, he couldn't even remember how to shift gears. Was second gear forward or back?

But there wasn't time to think about it. The other guys had already started their bikes, and were lining up facing the most winding part of the road.

I'll look like a total wimp if I drop out now, Dylan thought.

"There's a red piece of cloth hanging on the barricade at the west ramp," Neil said. "Winner brings it back. And hey, Dylan—hang tough, man."

The minute Dylan climbed on his bike, Neil raised his arm overhead and let it drop, signaling the start of the race.

Dylan's bike jumped forward, first off the line, spewing engine fumes into Billy's face. But a second later, Dylan felt the roar of the other bikers moving forward, surrounding him. Sure, Neil's bike was fast, but it was smaller than the others. It didn't have the kind of power the others had in the long stretch.

Mistake . . . major mistake, Dylan thought to himself. These guys are out to kill me . . .

But he just held on, revving the engine and running through all the gears. The speedometer hit 69 when suddenly one of the guys in black leather pulled up on the left and started shouting in Dylan's face.

"Move over! Move over!"

At least that's what it looked like he was saying. Dylan couldn't hear a thing over the blast of the motorcycle engines. What was this guy trying to do? Shove him off the road and into oblivion?

Dylan was slowing down, gripping the handlebars tighter as he tried to hold his position. Then suddenly the bike slid out from under him—the road was curving sharply to the left, banking slightly like the inside curve of a roller dome. And in that instant, Dylan realized why the other biker had been yelling at him to move over: he had been trying to save his life!

Dylan tried to lean with the bike, but it didn't make sense on this curve. In fact, Dylan realized, he was going much too fast to be in control—and that he had no idea how to take a curve like this on a motorcycle.

He tried to slow down, but in the next instant the bike skidded out from under him. He was totally out of control—aware only that he was falling, skidding, and finally crashing in a blur of smoke, noise, gravel, and pain.

I'm not wearing a helmet, he thought an instant before he hit the ground. It was his last conscious moment—the last thing he thought, right before his entire world went dark.

"No!" Billy cried out as he and Neil began running toward Dylan. "NO!"

The other bikers circled around and came back, just as Neil and Billy reached the spot where Dylan was lying on the side of the road.

"Don't touch him, man!" the guy in the yellow windbreaker said. "I'll go get help. I hope we can get him to the hospital."

Billy couldn't believe it. He looked at Dylan's lifeless body lying on the road. "I made him do it! He's dead and it's all my fault!" Billy shouted, as he ran off down the road.

CHAPTER 2

"**C**OURTNEY! WHERE *WERE* you last night? Something terrible has happened," Ashley said, coming up behind her best friend.

Ashley's soft voice startled Courtney, almost more than if she had spoken loudly—although Ashley *never* spoke loudly. She didn't seem to be capable of it.

"Don't sneak up on me like that," Courtney said, checking her long brown hair in the mirror mounted inside her locker door. "What happened that was so terrible?"

"Didn't Billy tell you?"

"Tell me what? I don't see Billy so much any-

more, now that he's living at Dad's apartment,"
Courtney said.

"I know," Ashley went on. "But I thought he
would have called you. *I* called and called until
11:30. Where *were* you?"

"My mom and I went to a movie and then had
a late pizza. I think she's still totally depressed
about the divorce. Why? What happened?"

"It's Dylan."

"Dylan?" Courtney's heart skipped a beat at
the mention of his name.

"He was riding a motorcycle yesterday after
school . . . and there was an accident . . . and
Dylan was hurt." Ashley's voice sounded even
softer, but strained.

"Dylan?" Courtney said it again and felt a
lump forming in her throat. Ashley nodded and
touched Courtney's arm.

"I know you still have feelings for him."

Still have feelings for Dylan? That was an
understatement, Courtney thought to herself.
Dylan was everything Courtney wanted in a guy.
He was talented, sensitive, vulnerable, and in-
credibly cute. Okay—so maybe he was a bit of a
rebel. But that just made him all the more attrac-
tive. Courtney felt like she *understood* Dylan,
maybe better than anyone else did. And on top of

everything else, Dylan was really nice to Billy, her younger brother. How could she help but love him for that?

"Is he all right? I mean, how badly hurt is he?"

"The doctors aren't sure. An ambulance brought him in yesterday while I was working my shift at the hospital. I couldn't get too many details because they won't tell you much when you're just a candy striper. But when I left, I think he was still unconscious."

"Oh, no," Courtney bit her bottom lip. "You mean he's in a coma?"

"I'm just not sure," Ashley said, letting her voice trail off.

The bell for first period rang, and Ashley slipped into a state of minor panic. "Oh, no, now I'm going to be late and Mr. Arthur will have a fit." Her soft voice rose in pitch.

She started pulling books out of her locker, her honey-blond hair swinging from side to side.

"I've got to go," she said, beginning to run down the hall. Then she stopped and turned to face Courtney again. "Oh, listen to me worrying about being late when Dylan is in the hospital. I'm sorry, Courtney. I promise—we'll talk later."

"Ashley!" Courtney said. "Wait a minute. How does Billy know about this?"

"Billy was with Dylan when it happened," she said.

"Oh, no! Why didn't you say so? Was Billy hurt too?"

"I don't think so. I don't have the details, but if Billy was hurt, I probably would have heard. Some guy named Neil rode with Dylan to the hospital and he said that Billy was there, and he was pretty upset. That's really all I know and now I'm *definitely* late for first period. I'm sorry Courtney, I've got to go."

The lump in Courtney's throat doubled in size and a terrible thought hit her like a brick in the stomach. Why hadn't Billy called her? Suddenly she had to find out where Billy was, and fast. She ran down the hall to his first period class—he did have math first period, didn't he? Yeah, that was right. Mr. Sigur's class.

Courtney looked in through the window on the closed door and scanned every face. Billy wasn't there.

Tears began to well up in Courtney's eyes. She tried to tell herself that Dylan would be fine and Billy was probably home. Everything was fine.

But something told her that just wasn't true. She hurried back to her locker, spun the combination quickly, threw her books back inside, and ran out of the school.

Now I'm cutting class, she thought to herself—just like Dylan.

But she wasn't just like Dylan—not that way—and she knew it. This was different. This wasn't cutting just to be cutting. This was an absolute crisis.

Courtney ran down the front steps of school and brushed past Matt on her way out. Apparently he was coming to school late.

"Courtney? What's wrong?" Matt asked, sounding really concerned.

"I can't explain now," she said, still running. "Have you seen Billy?"

Matt shook his head no. "Are you okay?" he called.

"I don't know," she called back. "Ask Ashley. She'll tell you all about it!"

Courtney dashed into the Avalon. It looked weird. She wasn't used to seeing it so empty. Usually the place was filled with people hanging out and eating burgers. But not at 9:00 in the morning. Right now, every single booth was deserted.

Frantically, Courtney dug through her purse for money.

"Can I have some change for the pay phone, please?" she asked the cashier, half out of breath.

"Don't you want something to eat? A blueberry muffin, maybe?"

It was a new cashier, a cute red-haired guy, who was trying to flirt. Normally Courtney would have been flattered, but this wasn't the time for it.

"It's an emergency," she said. "Could you please just give me some change?"

It took three phone calls to her mother and two to her father—one to his answering machine at his apartment and the other to his secretary at work—before she found out it was true. Billy was missing.

This is awful, Courtney thought to herself, remembering what Ashley had said. If only I'd been there . . . if only Billy had called me . . . if only our parents hadn't gotten divorced . . . then maybe this never would have happened.

The long and short of it was that her dad had been out of town last night on business, so he hadn't realized that Billy didn't come home. Actually, he *did* realize it—because he had called the apartment to check on Billy. But when he got the machine instead of Billy, he had just assumed that Billy was staying with Courtney and their mom instead.

It's true that Billy did that every once in a while. But Courtney could hear the anger in her mom's voice, and she knew what it meant. Her mom blamed her dad for not being home—for not knowing that Billy was gone. Great. Just what we needed, Courtney thought. More tension. Something *else* to fight about.

So now the police were called and they were out looking for Billy. Except that they probably wouldn't look very hard since it was official policy *not* to look until someone had been missing for twenty-four hours.

Courtney dropped the remaining coins into the bottom of her purse and left the Avalon. Now what?

She decided there was only one thing to do: go looking for Billy herself. She knew him so well, knew where he liked to go and what he liked to do. The only problem was that she couldn't think of many places to look. She and her brother spent almost all of their time in one of three spots: home, the Avalon, and school. Of course there was always the mall . . . But what were the chances that he'd be hanging out there at 9:00 in the morning? Was it even open?

No, there was only one place that really made sense, Courtney decided. The hospital. Maybe Billy was there! Maybe he came back to find out if Dylan was okay. And if not, at least Dylan might have some ideas about where Billy would go.

But as soon as Courtney thought about Dylan, her throat tightened up again. What if he was really badly hurt? Courtney's mind skipped back and forth. She had to find Billy! Maybe Dylan would know something. But would it do any good to ask him? According to Ashley, he was lying in a hospital bed—unconscious.

Unless he's awake now, Courtney thought, crossing her fingers again.

She patted her hair in place, making sure it hadn't gotten too messy. And then she felt guilty for even thinking that way. She shouldn't care about impressing Dylan at a time like this. Not with him so hurt and Billy still missing!

She hopped a bus across town and was at the hospital by 10:00 when visiting hours began.

Then she quickly walked up to the information desk and asked the gray-haired woman what room Dylan was in.

"Room 443, North Wing," the woman said pleasantly.

"Thank you," Courtney said. She turned to leave, then changed her mind and turned back. "Excuse me, but may I ask you another question? I'm looking for my brother and I wondered if you'd seen him, hanging around in the lobby or anything. He's blond, a little shorter than I am, fourteen years old—"

"Sorry," the woman said, interrupting. "I've only been on duty for an hour and I haven't seen anyone like that."

"Oh. Well, thanks."

Courtney rode the elevator to the fourth floor, and turned toward the North Wing, the part of the hospital that overlooked the lake. All the way down the hallway, she held on to the slim hope that Billy would already be there, visiting Dylan. She knocked lightly on the door, then pushed it open and went in.

"Dylan?" she called softly. "Oh, my god . . ."

He was so still, so immobile on the hard flat bed, and his skin was so pale that for half a second Courtney thought he was dead.

She walked toward the bed and stood a few feet away, not daring to come too close. His breathing was too shallow . . . in fact, was he breathing at all? Oh yeah, there was the monitor. They had him hooked up to some oxygen . . . and an IV tube was in his arm . . .

But Billy wasn't there. There was no one in sight.

"Excuse me, are you a member of the family?"

A brisk nurse came into the room like she owned the place, startling Courtney. She walked quickly to Dylan's bed to rearrange his covers.

"Uh, no . . . I'm just a friend . . ."

"Well, he shouldn't be disturbed. He needs his sleep. And morning visiting hours are over at noon—we're very strict about that for the patient's good."

"Oh, sure, I'll leave at 12:00. But, uh, can you tell me what's wrong with him? I mean, is he in a coma? Is he going to be all right?"

The nurse didn't make much effort to be quiet or gentle, and she didn't answer Courtney right away. She just rearranged the things on Dylan's nightstand, moving his phone further away and his water pitcher closer to him.

"He's not unconscious, just heavily sedated," the nurse finally said. "But you'll have to ask his doctor if you want any more information than that. I'm not allowed to disclose the details except to family members."

"But, I mean, is he going to be . . ." Courtney's voice trailed off. The nurse had already left the room.

"Well, Dylan, I'm here. If you can hear me . . ."

For the next five minutes, she stood at his side thinking about what it would be like if she and Dylan actually were going together. Dylan, the rebel who usually screwed up his life—going with Courtney, the leading candidate for Most Responsible Girl of the Year. They'd make a weird couple, that's for sure.

But if we *were* going together, she thought, she'd definitely have an excuse to sit by his bed every minute, holding his beautiful, sensitive hands and willing him to get better. Maybe she'd even read him some of her poetry when he was sleeping.

And then, when he finally woke up, he would reach up and pull her down to him, kissing her.

Suddenly, before Courtney knew what she was doing, she bent over his sleeping face and kissed him on the mouth . . .

She let her lips linger for a moment . . .

"Dylan," she whispered.

He moved slightly, and Courtney stepped back. Wake up, Dylan, she prayed. Please . . . wake up.

"Well, well, look who's here!"

A voice behind Courtney made her jump and turn around with a start. But even before she turned, she recognized the fake-sweet, snotty voice. Courtney knew that voice anywhere. It was Brooke.

CHAPTER 3

BROOKE WAS STANDING in the doorway, looking beautiful as usual and smiling her superior, phony smile that always looked like it said: "I caught you."

"Brooke! What are you doing here?"

"I brought Dylan's homework," Brooke said, although she didn't have any books in her hands. It was obvious that Brooke was only there to get some new Dylan gossip. "What are *you* doing here? Or shouldn't I ask?"

Courtney hesitated, wondering just how long Brooke had been standing there. Long enough to see her kiss Dylan? Or was she just trying to stir up trouble, as usual?

"I came to see if Dylan knew anything about my brother," Courtney said. "Billy's missing."

"I heard," Brooke said. "But then, don't you think you should be out looking for him?"

"I am. I mean, I *was*," Courtney sputtered, feeling caught again. "I mean, I told you. I thought Dylan might know where Billy was—or that Billy might have come here, to see Dylan."

"Whatever," Brooke said, tossing her hair as if she didn't believe a word Courtney said. "Anyway, I've got to get back to school before lunch is over. This is pretty hot news, don't you think?"

"What is?" Courtney held her breath. Had Brooke seen the kiss?

"About Dylan," Brooke said. "Lying here tragically wounded. I promised everyone at school that I'd find out how he was, so I'd better go."

Brooke turned to leave, but then hesitated for a moment and gave Courtney another mocking smile. "Coming?"

"Uh, sure," Courtney said, walking out of the room with Brooke. "But not back to school. I still have to find Billy."

But where am I going to look? Courtney thought to herself.

Dylan tried to roll over in bed, but the minute he moved, everything hurt.

What day was it?

Where . . . ?

Oh yeah, he vaguely remembered now. He was in the hospital. He'd been waking up and falling asleep, off and on, for the past two days, ever since the accident. And each time he woke up, he seemed to be able to *feel* a little more. More bruises, more scrapes, more pain.

And more memories. Those were the most painful of all. The motorcycle . . . the race . . . the crash. It was a blur, but he had a general idea of everything that happened.

Then Dylan remembered last night, with his parents coming in late, lecturing him. His dad was furious, especially about how much it was going to cost to pay for the hospital bills. And his mom just kept saying the same thing to his dad that she always said: "Forget it, honey. If he hasn't learned by now, he never will."

Fortunately, someone kept coming in and shooting him full of painkillers, so he could forget about all of that and sleep. From the throbbing pain in his head and wrist, he figured it was time for another dose now.

Maybe that's why someone was knocking on his door. Dylan tried to say "Come in," but his voice was too weak. He could barely be heard.

"Hey—knock, knock. You awake, man?"

The door swung open and Neil poked his head in. Dylan recognized his voice, even without looking up.

"Hi," Dylan said weakly.

Neil came in slowly, awkwardly, as if he felt out of place.

"So how you doin'?" Neil asked.

"Who knows?" Dylan tried to sit up, but he couldn't. Every muscle in his body had been bruised when he hit the pavement. He was lucky to be alive.

"So, uh—nice room," Neil said, looking around uncomfortably. The other bed in Dylan's room was empty, so Neil sat on it, facing Dylan, putting one foot up on the bed rails.

"How long have I been in here, anyway? What day is it?"

"It's Wednesday afternoon," Neil said. "Don't tell me you have amnesia, man! The accident was two days ago."

"I'm just sort of fogged out."

"That's good. 'Cause I don't think I could deal with any more guilt. I already feel bad enough about letting you in that race."

"No, it was my fault," Dylan said. "I wasn't ready for it. I feel like a jerk."

"Hey, forget it. Really. I shouldn't have let you ride. That road is such a grind, half the guys I know wipe out on that curve. It's just that you were such a hotshot on my bike the other times you rode it. Blew my mind!"

Dylan was quiet for a minute, staring at the wall and almost falling asleep again. He closed his eyes for a minute, then opened them and looked over at Neil.

"So how's your bike?" he asked.

"It's a mess," Neil said with an ironic laugh. "How's your head?"

"Hurts like mad. And they say my wrist is broken."

"Hey, I really am sorry, man."

"Forget it," Dylan said. "I told you. It's not your fault."

But it was hard for Dylan to forget about it— especially when he remembered what the doctors had said last night. A broken wrist would heal— but nerve damage was different. Unfortunately, there was no way to tell—not yet—whether any nerves *had* been damaged.

And that meant there was no way to know whether Dylan would ever be able to play the guitar again.

Dylan could hardly stand to think about it. He closed his eyes tight, to shut out the idea. What would he do if he couldn't play the guitar? Music was the only thing he had ever been good at! Everything else in his life was a mess—a complete and total mess. Now the only escape from these terrible thoughts—and the pain—was sleep. And without saying another word to Neil, Dylan drifted off.

Neil sat and watched Dylan for about ten minutes. Then, just when he was about to leave, the door to Dylan's room opened wider and Ashley walked in. Her pale blond hair was held off her face with a pink headband that matched her pink and white candy striper uniform.

Seconds later, Dylan opened his eyes. "Hi, Dylan," she said softly. "How are you? I mean, are you feeling any better?"

"Actually I feel worse," Dylan said. "My head is killing me. And my wrist—" He cradled it with his good hand to indicate how sore it was.

"I'm sorry to hear that," Ashley said in her

most sympathetic voice. "Maybe some visitors will cheer you up. Look who I brought with me."

On cue, Courtney stepped into the room from the hallway and flashed her best smile at Dylan.

"Hi," she said, trying to convey as much sympathy and adoration as possible, without overdoing it.

"Hi, Courtney," Dylan said. He gave her a warm smile back, as if he were glad to see her. "What's up?"

Courtney's first thought was of Billy. His running away was certainly news. But she didn't want to bring it up just yet. It might upset Dylan too much.

"What's up with *me?*" Courtney said, trying to smile. "You're the one with the news. Everyone at school is talking about your accident."

"Oh, great," Dylan said. "More gossip about me. The troublemaker gets what he deserves. Just what I need."

"Oh, no, it's nothing like that," Courtney said quickly. "You know what they're saying—just how awful it is, how everyone's worried about you, how you might have been killed. Stuff like that."

"Oh," Dylan said.

"Everyone misses you—even Jerry, the waiter

at the Avalon was asking about you," Courtney added.

Dylan frowned. "Don't mention the Avalon."

"Why not?"

"I was supposed to give a concert there next month. But now . . ." His voice trailed off and he looked down at his broken wrist.

Oh, no, Courtney thought. Was he saying he wouldn't be able to play? Courtney suddenly realized that she *still* didn't know just how serious his injuries were. All she knew was that she had to say something to cheer him up, something to change that absolutely miserable expression on his face.

"Listen, Dylan. I'm *sure* your wrist will get better sooner or later. I mean, maybe it won't be in time for the Avalon . . . but eventually you'll be able to play the guitar again . . . won't you?"

"Who knows?" Dylan shrugged.

"Well, it just *has* to get better," Courtney went on being positive. "I mean, lots of athletes break their wrists and come back from it—so you can, too."

"Well, yeah, maybe . . ." But he didn't sound convinced. "Anyway, thanks for the pep talk," Dylan said, giving Courtney a special smile of real gratitude. For a moment, their eyes locked and she felt as if they were the only two people in the room.

Then she remembered—they weren't alone. Ashley and Neil were talking quietly by the window.

"Listen, Dylan," she said softly. "There's something important I wanted to ask you. My brother's been missing ever since your accident. Do you have any idea where he could be?"

Dylan shook his head. "Billy? Missing? Poor kid—I had no idea. I hope he's okay. But I don't know what happened. Why would I?"

"I just thought maybe he came to visit you— to see if you were okay. Or maybe you'd have an idea about where he might go, since he hangs out with you so much."

Dylan sort of shrugged and Courtney could see that he wasn't really strong enough or clear-headed enough for this kind of conversation. He was still too dopey from the medications they were giving him.

"It's just that I've been looking for him for two days," Courtney explained, turning to Ashley. "What am I going to do? I tried the mall . . . the Avalon. I even went over to Dylan's garage to see if he was there, but no luck."

"Try the mall again," Ashley suggested. "It's warm and dry, and you can get something to eat there. That's where I'd probably go if I wanted to just hang out by myself for awhile." Then Ashley looked at her watch. "Uh-oh. Dylan is supposed to be getting some X rays now." She turned on her heel. "The nursing staff is short today, so I have to find an orderly. Be right back!"

Less than a minute later Ashley was back, pushing an empty wheelchair in front of her. "Can you help this patient into the wheelchair?" she called to an orderly in the hall.

"I can do it myself," Dylan said weakly. But it was obvious he didn't have the strength. The orderly half-lifted Dylan into the wheelchair and a moment later he and Ashley wheeled Dylan out of the room.

Courtney found herself standing alone with Neil. She hoped he would leave, but it didn't look promising. He started playing with the thin box of tissues on Dylan's nightstand, tossing it in the air and catching it, over and over.

"So. How long have you known Dylan?" she finally asked, breaking the silence.

"Long time," Neil said. "It was my bike he was riding when he got hurt."

"Really? Did you see my brother Billy after the accident?" Courtney asked.

"That was your brother? That kid who came with Dylan?"

Courtney nodded. "And he's been missing

ever since. Do you have *any* idea where he might have gone?''

Neil shook his head. "The whole thing happened like lightning," he said. "Dylan's bike went down, and Billy and I started running toward Dylan. Then this guy I know, Gary, tore off on his bike to get help. At first, we couldn't tell how badly Dylan was hurt. We all thought he might be dead. Anyway we didn't want to move him, so we just threw a few more jackets on top of him and waited for the paramedics."

"Did Billy say anything?"

"Yeah, he said something like 'It's my fault. I made him go.' "

"That's terrible," Courtney said, picturing it. "It wasn't Billy's fault. He didn't *make* Dylan race."

"Nah—he just sort of urged him to do it. But so did I."

"That doesn't make it anyone's fault," Courtney said.

"Yeah, well, he's a kid, right?" Neil shrugged as if that explained everything. "Anyway, the paramedics came pretty quick, and said Dylan was going to be okay. But Billy had already run off. He left the accident before the paramedics even arrived."

"Oh, no," Courtney said, suddenly realizing what Billy had thought. "So he left before he found out that Dylan was okay?"

"Yeah."

"Oh, no," Courtney moaned again.

"I feel pretty bad about the whole thing. I mean, it was my bike . . . now Dylan's hurt . . . your brother's missing. What a mess."

Neil looked away and Courtney watched him out of the corner of her eye. He seemed genuinely upset, and Courtney was surprised.

"Anyway, I've got to get to work," Neil said, hopping off the metal cabinet he had been perching on. "Tell Dylan I'll catch him later."

"Sure," Courtney said softly.

When he was gone, she sat down on Dylan's bed, running her hand over his sheets, the sheets where he had been lying just a few minutes before. She put her feet up on the edge of the bed railing and looked around the room, trying to imagine what it was like to be in the hospital.

Then she picked up the phone and dialed her mom.

"Hi, Mom," Courtney said. "It's me. I just found out something about Billy."

Quickly, Courtney told her mother that Billy urged Dylan to race the motorcycle and then left the accident blaming himself, probably thinking Dylan was dead.

When they hung up, Courtney sat for a minute longer, trying to think of other places Billy might have gone. The obvious places were out. The police were keeping an eye on the malls, the Avalon . . .

And Courtney's mom had called her grandmother and all of their other relatives. And Billy's friends. Several times. Everyone promised they'd call if they heard anything.

"Hey—scoot over and make room for me."

Courtney looked up and saw Dylan sitting there in his wheelchair, with Ashley behind him.

"Sorry," she stammered, hopping out of his bed.

"That's okay," he said, really smiling. He seemed to be in a much better mood.

Courtney and Ashley helped Dylan back into bed, making sure he didn't fall.

"I've got to go," Ashley said after that. "I'm supposed to be delivering mail and flowers right now, and I'm late. See you later!" With that, she sped out of the room.

Courtney waited while Dylan got comfortable on the hospital bed. She could see, from the way he was still holding his wrist, that he was in pain.

"I've never broken anything," Courtney said. "It looks like it really hurts, huh?"

"Yeah," Dylan said. "It does." Then, to her surprise, he reached out his injured hand and took her hand in his.

"Courtney . . . could you hold my hand? Just for a minute," he said.

Courtney's heart raced as he closed his fingers tightly around hers. Could this really be happening? Was he really trying to tell her he liked her? She felt like she could barely breathe.

Dylan started to let go, then squeezed her hand tightly again. A warm feeling washed through her whole body, so warm it made her want to faint.

This was even better than the kiss she gave Dylan when he was sleeping, Courtney thought— or at least almost as good. Because this was *Dylan*, wide awake and telling her how *he* felt about her! Letting her in to his most private feelings—into his secret life.

No matter how reckless he was, no matter what other people thought of him, Courtney was going to stand by him, she decided.

Dylan was worth it, and besides—she had to admit that she had already fallen deeply, dangerously in love.

CHAPTER 4

IN GYM CLASS the next day, Courtney was running around the track. She was in a world of her own. A private, lonely world that was rocketing out of control.

It was four days now since the accident, and Billy still hadn't been found. The police were looking for him full time, but even they admitted that it was practically impossible to find a runaway teenager who didn't want to be found.

Meanwhile Courtney had promised her mother that she'd go to school . . . go to her classes . . . try to act normal. But how could she act normal when everything was such a mess? Not only was Billy missing, but Dylan was still in the hospital. Courtney wanted to help both of them—and there was nothing she could do for either one.

How can you even think about Dylan when your brother is gone? Courtney asked herself. But even running five laps around the track didn't take Courtney's mind off Dylan. Especially not when she thought about what happened yesterday . . . when he held her hand.

She ran the final lap, then headed into the locker room and took a shower, completely lost in her own thoughts, unaware that anyone else was around.

After her shower, she checked her hair in the locker room mirror, tugging in frustration at the wisps that were still wet.

It'd better be dry by the time school's out, she thought to herself. Because I'm not going to visit Dylan in the hospital looking like this!

"Oh, trying a new hairstyle, are we?"

Suddenly that fake-sweet, snotty voice was there again. Courtney turned around and found Brooke standing behind her trying to look innocent. Which for Brooke, was practically impossible.

"I mean, how did your hair get so *wet?*" Brooke went on, full of phony sympathy.

"It's called taking a shower, Brooke. Why isn't *your* hair wet?" Courtney asked although she already knew the answer. Brooke had cut gym again, for about the fiftieth time, using some lame excuse from her mom or her doctor.

"Oh, I wish I *could* take gym," Brooke said, "so I could stay in shape like you do."

Courtney knew Brooke didn't really mean that as a compliment, but she ignored it anyway.

"Does my hair really look that bad?" Courtney asked.

"Why? Are you going someplace special?"

Courtney blushed. "No—I mean, I'm just going to the hospital to see Dylan after school."

"Oh, dear."

"What?"

"Well, are you sure you want to do that? I mean, I just hope he doesn't hurt you again, like he did the last time you went chasing after him."

"Chasing?" Courtney dropped the comb she had been holding. "As I remember, *you* were the one who was chasing after him."

"Don't be ridiculous," Brooke said, tossing her short hair haughtily. "I have never been the least bit interested in Dylan."

"Then why did you spend so much time hanging around his garage?"

"I was simply trying to learn more about his music," Brooke lied. "As a matter of fact, at the time, I was considering a singing career."

Courtney knew this wasn't true, and she also knew that if she spent much more time arguing with Brooke, she'd be late to class. So she dropped the subject completely.

"I've got to go," Courtney said, gathering up her books. "See you later."

"Yes," Brooke said. "I *will* see you later."

There wasn't time to wonder what that meant. Courtney had to hurry to avoid getting another of what Mr. Franklin called his "booby points." Whenever you made a mistake of any kind in his class, he gave you a booby point—for making a boo-boo, he explained. Everyone thought he was such a jerk, and his point system was so idiotic, that everyone tried hard not to get points, just to avoid hearing him use that word. The really stupid part was that getting booby points didn't even affect your grade. He just gave the points to embarrass people.

The next two hours seemed to drag on forever. The only good thing about it was that it was long enough for Courtney's hair to dry. By the time she headed for the hospital after school, the wispy parts of hair were framing her face nicely. In fact, Courtney thought it looked so good, maybe she'd let it dry naturally like this from now on.

"I know!" Courtney said out loud as she got to the hospital. She had just gotten a brilliant idea. Flowers! What a great, romantic gesture, to take Dylan some flowers. Something to make him think of her, every time he looked at them.

Courtney stopped in the florist shop in the hospital lobby and bought a mixed bouquet of mums, daisies, and baby's breath, tied with a rubber band, and wrapped in a paper cone. Compared to the roses, tulips, and freesia in the refrigerator case, it wasn't a very pretty mix. But it was all she could afford. And anyway, Courtney thought, who else will bring him flowers? It's the thought that counts.

But the minute she walked into his room, she saw how wrong she had been. The place was filled with get-well cards and flowers, all of them more beautiful than the pitiful little bouquet in her hands! There were four different arrangements crowded together on his window ledge, and a huge green vase of red roses on the nightstand right next to his bed. Instinctively, her arm jerked to hide her own flowers behind her back, but it wasn't necessary, because Dylan's bed was empty. He was gone.

Gone? No—his sheets were messed up and his clothes were still there. He was probably just getting an X ray or something, Courtney thought. She looked around for a place to put her flowers, and then she felt even more embarrassed. There wasn't a container in sight. Not even a glass large enough to hold the bouquet.

What a jerk, Courtney said to herself. Everyone else sent flowers that came in their own vases or containers. She felt so dumb for not thinking of that.

Oh well, I'll just make the best of it, she thought. It *was* the thought that counted, wasn't it?

And maybe, since she had a few minutes to herself, she could think of something clever to write on the card. Something that would make her simple gift seem better than these other enormous flower arrangements . . .

How about: To Dylan, who lives mostly on the dark side . . . Look what can bloom if you'll only let in a little light!

No—that sounded like a lecture.

How about: To Dylan—Here are some *mums*,

because I know you don't like to talk about yourself . . . Some daisies, so that you'll always know "She loves you" . . . and some baby's breath because . . . because . . .

Because what? This was stupid and going nowhere, Courtney decided.

How about: To Dylan, Simple flowers for a simply fabulous guy . . .

Yuk! Maybe it was better to just forget the flowers. Who were these other bouquets from, anyway? Courtney was half-tempted to read the cards and find out.

She walked over to the roses first, hoping that the name on the card would be showing or lying on the nightstand or something. But it wasn't. It was still in its envelope, pinned to the green ribbon encircling the vase.

How about the other arrangements? Same thing. The cards hadn't been opened yet. Apparently these flowers had all just arrived. Either that, or Dylan was such a loner, he didn't even want to know who they were from!

Oh well, Courtney thought. She certainly wasn't going to read his mail before he did.

"Snooping around, are we?"

That voice. Brooke, again! What was she doing here?

Courtney whirled around and saw Brooke standing in the doorway, holding a box of candy tied with a red satin ribbon. She looked fabulous, as usual, wearing her shortest, tightest, black skirt and a pale green cashmere sweater. The pale green color made Brooke's hair look like copper. Courtney looked down at the flowers, still clutched in her hand, and felt totally out of place.

"No, I was *not* snooping around," Courtney said. "I was just looking for a place to put these flowers, for Dylan."

"Oh, I knew everyone would bring flowers, so I brought candy instead," Brooke said in her most superior tone. "Are those, well . . . from your *own garden* or something?"

Courtney wanted to die, but she was determined not to let Brooke get to her.

"What are you doing here, anyway?" Courtney asked. "Two hours ago you said you had no interest in Dylan."

"I don't have any *romantic* interest in him," Brooke said. "But as a friend and a compassionate person, I of course wanted to show him that I understand what he's going through. Hmmm, I wonder who sent him the roses? Let's open the card."

"We can't do that," Courtney said. She tried

to block the way, but Brooke was moving pretty fast.

"Who's going to stop us?"

"That's not right, Brooke," Courtney said weakly. But even to herself, Courtney thought she sounded unsure. And anyway, what could she do? Brooke was already opening the envelope right in front of Courtney's eyes.

"Now, let's see who his biggest fan is," Brooke said as she whipped something out of the envelope. It turned out to be a piece of paper, folded several times to fit where a small cardboard gift card would normally go. There was a silence as Brooke unfolded it and read it to herself, her mouth slowly falling open.

Courtney could hardly stand the suspense, but she didn't want to come right out and ask who it was from.

"Well? Anyone we know?" she finally said.

"You aren't going to believe this. You are simply *not* going to believe this!" Brooke squealed. She handed the note to Courtney, who hesitated only a fraction of a second before reading it herself. It said:

I'm sorry to hear about your accident, even if I *am* angry with you. Your son misses you—

you never visit him. In fact, you act
like he doesn't exist! Well, he *does*
exist, and I'm bringing him to the hospital to visit you—as soon as you're
well enough. So prepare yourself! *Lisa*

Your *son?* Courtney read the words over three
times, her heart pounding painfully in her chest.

She was stunned. Dylan? A father? Dylan had
a son? It was more than she could comprehend.
No wonder he keeps to himself so much! No wonder he acts like he has something to hide!

"I don't believe this," Courtney said weakly.

"Neither do I," Brooke said, sounding
shocked. "It's just *soooo* amazing. Amazing but
typical of our Dylan. Can you believe he's been
able to hide it so well for all these months? Or dare
I say years?"

Courtney shuddered at the thought. It was
bad enough, imagining Dylan had a child. That he
had a secret life. But the idea that he was a father!
It was too much.

Courtney wanted to cry, but not in front of
Brooke. Never in front of Brooke.

"Isn't this too good to be true?" Brooke went
on, her excitement building. She was obviously
delighted with the news. "But who, I wonder, is
this Lisa person?"

"I have no idea," Courtney managed to say through the lump in her throat.

"Me neither. There aren't any Lisas at school. No *important* Lisas, anyway."

"So then who can it be?"

"I just can't imagine. It must be an *older woman*," Brooke said pointedly. "Someone more experienced than, well . . . anyone we know. All I know is that this is the hottest news I've heard in *months*, and it's my duty to let my friends know. So that they don't throw themselves at someone who's, well, already taken."

Brooke grabbed the note from Courtney's hand.

"What are you doing?" Courtney said, her voice rising.

"I might need this as evidence," Brooke said, putting the note in her purse. "In case anyone doubts this incredible story and wants to see the proof."

"Wait!" Courtney tried to run after her. But what was the point? Brooke was clearly determined to spread this gossip all over school. And once Brooke decided to do something, there was no stopping her.

CHAPTER 5

BROOKE BREEZED INTO the photocopy store as if she owned it, with Dylan's secret pressed into her hand. There was a long line of people waiting at the counter, and only one self-serve copy machine. A gray-haired man in a brown tweed coat and wire-rimmed glasses was using it, his papers spread all over the top.

"Excuse me, but are you going to be very long?" Brooke said to him, using a syrupy-sweet little-girl voice.

"No, I'm just about through," he said.

"Well," Brooke said, checking the clock on the back wall, "I only have this one little thing to copy . . ." And if I don't hurry, she thought to herself, the Avalon will be practically empty by the time I get there!

She held up the tiny folded note from Dylan's roses.

"Do you mind?" she said.

The man looked unwilling to move all his papers, but Brooke gave him such a stare that he finally said okay.

"Thank you so much," Brooke said, setting the machine for thirty copies. The man glared at her as the slow machine scanned the note and flashed its light, thirty times.

By the time she was through, it was almost 5:00 P.M. She grabbed the copies of Dylan's note and dashed toward the Avalon, stopping outside to fix her hair and makeup before going inside.

Oh, good, Brooke thought when she saw her ex-friend, Kelly sitting in a booth, doing homework. Kelly and Brooke used to be best friends. But then Brooke pulled one stunt too many—with Kelly as the target. Now Kelly was more suspicious of Brooke than anyone else was. She was smart—too smart to be fooled by Brooke's tricks and lies.

"Kel!" Brooke called, just oozing best-friendship. "Am I glad to see you."

"Hi, Brooke," Kelly said half-heartedly.

"Kelly, I think I deserve a better greeting than that—especially since I've chosen *you* to be the very first person to hear the most *incredible* news."

"What news?"

"Kelly, you're going to have to sound a little more interested than that."

"Okay, Brooke. *What* news?"

"This," Brooke said, whipping out one of the photocopies of Dylan's note. Then, before Kelly even had time to read it, Brooke told her the whole story.

"Dylan—a father?"

"I was as shocked as you are," Brooke said. "But here's the evidence. Don't you think it's our duty to spread the word—so that other girls won't get hurt by him in the same way?"

Kelly gave Brooke a sideways stare. "You'd better handle that part," Kelly said finally. "You're so much better at spreading news than I am."

Brooke shrugged, tossed her head, and pranced over to another table. Oh well, Brooke thought, I guess she's right. I *am* good at this!

Courtney was shaking as she watched Brooke

grab the note and run out of the hospital. Still trembling, she got into the hospital elevator and rode down to the ground floor.

There was no way to get over this. Dylan! A father? She just couldn't believe it.

And then the really awful part hit her right in the middle of her stomach. What was he thinking when he held her hand yesterday? What did *he* think it meant?

Just then the elevator doors opened. As Courtney got out in the lobby, a young woman and her baby got in. Courtney's heart skipped a beat.

Was that Lisa? With Dylan's son?

Suddenly Courtney felt crazed with curiosity. She just *had* to know.

Instantly, she stuck her hand in the closing elevator doors. The doors jerked open again, and Courtney jumped back inside.

"I, uh, forgot something. Upstairs," she pointed up nervously, trying to explain her weird behavior.

The woman ignored Courtney and played with one of her earrings in her left ear. She looked like she was about 20 or 21 and the baby was about a year old. He was walking, but just barely. After a minute, she picked him up and held him in her arms.

Courtney tried to sneak a sideways glance, to check out the details. Short, spiky black hair with a thin purple streak in front . . . four earrings in one ear . . . oversized black sweater and skintight black pants . . . *Please* don't let this be the one, Courtney thought. How could she ever compete with someone like that?

Then the elevator doors opened again and the woman got out. It was the third floor.

Yea! Wrong floor! Not Dylan's child at all! Courtney was so relieved, she wanted to grab someone and tell them the good news. Dylan was on the fourth floor in the North Wing, so this was all just a stupid waste of time.

Except that it wasn't a waste of time, Courtney thought as she stepped off the elevator. Because somehow it made her realize how much she cared about Dylan. Even now. No matter what he'd done. She looked down at the droopy bouquet of flowers she was still carrying and smiled.

"Courtney? Are you okay?" Ashley's voice came from behind, startling her.

"Oh, hi. Yeah, I'm okay. Sort of."

"Well, are you lost? Dylan's on four, you know."

"Yeah, I know. No, I'm not lost. I'm just about to go into shock, I think."

"Why? What's wrong?"

"I can't tell you here."

"Why not?"

"Because it's serious. Very serious. Listen, do you have to candy stripe right now or can we go somewhere to get some soda and talk?"

Ashley looked at her watch and a guilty expression crept across her face. But then she forced herself to relax.

"Okay. I'll take fifteen minutes off. It won't kill me to abandon the magazine cart for a little while," she said. Then she pushed the cart to a spot at the end of the hallway, out of the way, and they rode the elevator to the basement.

They found a seat in the hospital cafeteria and sat down with two sodas. But Courtney just stirred hers. She was too upset to drink.

"So what's this about?" Ashley asked. "Do you have any news about Billy?"

"No, I wish I did," Courtney said. "This is about Dylan." Courtney paused. "I don't know how to say it."

"Well just try," Ashley said, getting slightly impatient.

"Okay, okay. I'll get to the point. It's just so hard to say." She stirred her soda some more. "You aren't going to believe this, but here goes.

Dylan has a child. A son."

Ashley put her hand to her mouth, and her pale skin turned paler. "Are you kidding? I mean, are you sure? I mean, how do you know?"

"I was in his room, and Brooke came in, and—".

"Oh, Courtney, if it's just something Brooke told you, forget it. You know she's such a liar."

"It's not something she told me. Just listen. Brooke read one of the cards that came with some roses for Dylan. It was from someone named Lisa, and it said 'your son misses you.' I saw it myself."

"That's all? Just 'your son misses you'?"

"No. The card said something about Dylan denying he had a son, or acting like he didn't have a son. And then it said she was going to bring him to the hospital to visit Dylan!"

"Oh, Courtney, that's awful. You're right—I don't believe it."

"Now do you see why I'm such a wreck?"

Ashley nodded, tilting her head to the side slightly. "So what are you going to do?"

"I don't know. What *should* I do?"

"Are you still in love with him?"

"I think so. I don't know. I'm pretty confused."

"Well," Ashley said slowly. "All I can tell you

is I've gone through some pretty rough times with Matt. But it never stopped me from loving him."

"So are you saying it's the same thing with me and Dylan?"

"Well, maybe. I think if you love someone, you should stand by him in the bad times, not just the good. Except that you and Dylan aren't . . . I mean, you aren't really . . ."

"You're saying we aren't really a couple." Courtney sounded hurt, but she knew it was the truth.

"Well, not yet. Not really. *Are* you?"

"Well, not really, but—"

Courtney told Ashley about what happened the day before in Dylan's room when he held her hand, and Ashley said it was great, giving Courtney a supportive smile. But they both knew it was just a beginning. The fact that Dylan squeezed her hand *still* didn't make it a relationship.

"I've got to go," Ashley said apologetically.

"Don't tell anyone," Courtney said.

"Of course I won't. But what difference would it make? Brooke has probably told half the school by now."

Courtney nodded. "I know. She even took the note with her—as proof."

"She did?"

"Yeah," said Courtney. "I tried to stop her but she ran out of the room."

"Yeah. Well, it *is* pretty amazing news." Ashley looked at her watch. "Sorry, I really do have to go. I'll call you later."

Courtney sat and stared at her soda as Ashley walked away. Now what? It was hard to know what to do next, let alone what to feel. Maybe Ashley was right . . . she and Dylan weren't really a couple—yet. But at least Ashley had said "yet." Maybe there was still hope.

And anyway Courtney couldn't abandon Dylan now, while he was at his weakest, lying in bed with his wrist broken. Not now when everyone in the whole school was going to be gossiping about him.

Poor Dylan, Courtney thought, remembering the note from Lisa. He doesn't even know what's going to hit him! He doesn't know that Lisa is coming, since Brooke took the note.

She'd better warn him, she decided. But first things first. She had to find out if there was any news about Billy. He'd been missing for four days now, and every hour that ticked by made the lump in Courtney's throat feel just a little bit larger.

Between Billy and Dylan, Courtney thought

she was going to go out of her mind.

They'll find Billy, she thought. They *have* to. But the feeling of desperation wouldn't go away, and it made her heart pound faster. Meanwhile, the awful thought kept creeping back in. What if they don't?

Courtney left her untouched drink sitting on the table and hurried to a pay phone to call home. But as soon as she heard her mom's voice, she knew the answer. There was no news about Billy. Well, Courtney thought, at least no news was supposed to be good news. Wasn't it?

For a minute she considered going to look for Billy some more. But the police had said to let them handle it. Courtney and her parents had been making themselves crazy, searching Hillside and neighboring towns, calling all of Billy's friends every few hours. The best thing Courtney could do now was to stay sane—so she'd be able to help out if her mom's anxiety went over the edge.

In a way, it was a relief to have this Dylan problem to worry about. It kept her mind off Billy, at least for a short while.

I've got to tell him who the roses are from, Courtney thought again. It's not fair that he doesn't know.

She rode the elevator back to the fourth floor, still carrying her own wilted bouquet of mums, and trying to figure out how to tell Dylan about the note. When she got there, his door was standing slightly ajar. She pushed it open slowly and peeked in.

"Dylan?"

"Oh, hi," he said, looking up with a tired expression on his face.

"Can I come in?"

"Sure. Why not?"

"How are you? I mean, are you any better?"

"My wrist still hurts, and I've got a killer headache. But everything else is a little better."

"Oh, well *that's* really good."

"Yeah, except—"

"What?"

"They still don't know whether there's any nerve damage."

"Oh." Courtney didn't know what to say. She cared about him, and she cared about his wrist getting better. But it seemed like the least of her problems right then.

"Listen, Dylan, there's something important I have to tell you—"

Her voice trailed off as she suddenly realized

what he had in his hand. It was one of the roses Lisa had sent him. Then she realized that he had been sniffing it when she walked in.

Did he know that the roses were from Lisa? Was he still hung up on her?

"Uh, nice flowers," she said, trying to sound casual. "Who are they from?"

"What these?" Dylan said. He sniffed the rose again. "I don't know. There was no card."

"Oh," Courtney said slowly. "Well . . . I mean, do you have any idea who might have sent them?"

"Not really," Dylan said. "I only got roses once—but that was a long time ago." His voice was trailing off, as if he were remembering something in the past.

"From who?"

"Just someone I knew."

"A girl?"

"Yeah—as a matter of fact. It was."

Lisa, Courtney thought. It had to be.

"What happened? I mean, were you in the hospital then, too?"

"No." Dylan paused, like he was deciding whether to tell her or not. "It was someone I went out with for a while," he said finally. "Someone really special. She was three years older than me, though, and her parents were rich and I think they hated my guts. Anyway, one time when they were out of town, I was over at her house. We were just watching TV when they came home—sooner than we thought." He paused again and Courtney held her breath. "They were totally furious when they saw us together. After that, they sent her to a different school."

A different school? Courtney knew what that meant. It *was* Lisa—it had to be.

And he was obviously still in love with her, from the faraway look on his face.

"Anyway," Dylan went on, "she sent me roses to say good-bye."

"Oh," Courtney said, trying to keep her voice steady. But her bottom lip was trembling. "Well, maybe these roses are from her, then."

"I doubt it," Dylan said.

"I don't." Tears were welling up in her eyes. "Anyway *I* brought you some flowers, too!" she said, almost crying. With a snap of her wrist, she threw the droopy bouquet of mums and daisies on his bed. Then she turned and ran out of the room.

CHAPTER 6

WHAT DID I say? Dylan wondered as Courtney stomped out of his hospital room, tossing some flowers on his bed as she left.

And why does this always happen to me?

With certain girls—and Courtney was one of them—Dylan was always somehow saying the wrong thing. He had hurt Courtney's feelings in the past, without meaning to, and apparently he had just done it again. He felt like a jerk.

Dylan went over the conversation in his head, trying to figure out what it was this time.

She was the one who had brought up the roses, wasn't she? And she was the one who asked about his old girlfriend. It's not like he started telling her all that stuff out of the blue. Maybe *Courtney* had brought the roses and expected him to know it. But that couldn't be. Or why would she have brought these?

Dylan picked up the flowers Courtney had brought and looked at them, smiling. It was really nice of her, he thought.

He looked around at all the flowers and cards decorating his hospital room. First he looked at the vase of roses, then at the bigger arrangements on the window ledge. It felt good to know that so many people cared about him.

One flower arrangement was from his guitar teacher, Mr. Patz. Then there were flowers from his family—his grandmother in Pittsburgh, an aunt in Detroit. None from his parents, of course. What did they care what happened to him? His parents had practically told him that they'd given up on him—for good.

Unless . . . maybe . . . what if the roses were from them? Wouldn't that be amazing? Deep down inside, Dylan hoped the roses *were* from his parents. Just once it would be nice if they showed they cared.

But what were the chances of that?

Dylan's head started to throb again and he

closed his eyes, ready to fall back to sleep. But then quickly he opened them again.

Wait a minute. Back up, Dylan thought. What had Courtney started to say? That there was something *really important* she had to tell him. What was it?

Oh—maybe it was something about Billy.

Yeah, that was probably it. And that's probably why she was so upset, too. About Billy. And who can blame her? What a mess! I just hope the kid's okay, Dylan thought, as he drifted off to sleep.

"Have you heard about Dylan?"

Courtney sighed and looked at Matt disapprovingly. He was the eleventh person to try to tell her about Dylan that day, and it was only second period on Friday morning. Courtney was keeping track. She made a little red X on the outside of her notebook, adding Matt to the count.

"Yes, Matt. I've *heard*. The whole school has heard by now. But don't you think we ought to respect his privacy a little bit?"

"Oh, right," Matt sneered. "Respect the privacy of Mr. Rebel. What a joke!"

"I don't see what's so funny about it."

"Using the word 'respect' in the same sentence with Dylan's name—*that's* what's so funny!" Matt's voice was as harsh as he could possibly make it. He and Dylan were so different. Always had been, always would be.

"How would you feel if the whole school talked about you and your problems?"

"My problems are *nothing* compared to what Dylan's done. This conversation's over," Matt announced, slamming his locker.

Fine, Courtney thought. Just please let me get through this day. For some reason, she felt like Dylan's scandal reflected badly on her, because everyone knew she liked him.

"Courtney, have you heard anything about—"

Courtney twirled around and saw Arseman standing behind her. Arseman, who was so smart, so level-headed, and usually so kind. Was she going to start trashing Dylan now, too?

"Have I heard *what?*" Courtney snapped.

"Have you heard anything about Billy? Did he come home yet?"

Billy! Courtney let out a long breath. All her doubts about Dylan were swept aside as she thought about her brother. "No, he hasn't come home. The police are still looking for him and my mom is going totally out of her mind. Thanks for asking, though."

"Well, you looked so tense. I've been worried about you. What did you think I was going to say, anyway?"

"Oh, I thought you were going to be the twelfth person to tell me the BIG NEWS about Dylan. I'm just sick of hearing everyone talk about him, that's all."

"Oh, that. Yeah, I've heard about it. But it just sounds like a lot of ugly gossip to me. How do we know it's true?"

I *know* it's true, Courtney thought to herself.

Arseman gave her a little squeeze on the arm. "Hey—cheer up. These things always blow over. And I'll bet Billy is just hiding out somewhere, waiting to be found. Worry about the pop quiz in Franklin's class instead. I had it first period and it's a killer. Fifty questions—and he calls that a *quiz!*"

Arseman looked so confident when she mentioned Billy, it was hard for Courtney not to smile.

"Thanks," she said.

But in her head she flashed on what the police

told her mom last night. Most missing kids were home within a day or two. Today was the fifth day since Billy disappeared. If Billy wasn't found soon, the chances of finding him went down to practically nil.

Courtney went to Mr. Franklin's class and tried to clear her head for the history quiz. And for a while it worked. The test kept her busy for about fifteen minutes, concentrating on names and dates and places. But she was such a good student that it really wasn't a very hard test. She finished before everyone else. Everyone, that is, except Ashley.

Courtney went back to thinking about Billy . . . and Dylan . . . and Lisa. Then she took out a sheet of paper and wrote a note to Ashley.

Ashley,
    I have to talk to you! I know I *should* forget all about Dylan—especially after finding out about his other life. But he looks so helpless in that hospital bed. I can't stop thinking about him—or Billy. The police still haven't found him. What if something *really* happened to him? Call me!!!!
                                    Courtney

Ashley read the note and wrote a reply on the back.

Courtney,
    Try not to worry about Billy. I'm sure he's fine. And I think Dylan really does like you. He always looks happier when you're there. But how can you get involved with someone who has a baby?! We'll talk later.
                                    — Ashley

Was that true, Courtney wondered? Did Dylan look happier when she was there? Actually, come to think of it, his eyes *did* seem to light up whenever she came into his room.

There was hope for her yet!

Courtney looked down at her test paper and realized that she had been writing Dylan's name in the margin, over and over again.

What am I doing? she wondered, feeling guilty all over again. How can I even think about Dylan, with Billy still gone?

Ashley knocked on Dylan's door and waited for him to answer before going in.

As a candy striper, she didn't usually knock first. She had been trained to simply enter each room quietly, without knocking, just like the doctors and nurses did. To deliver the mail to the 135 patients in less than an hour, she didn't have *time* to knock.

But with Dylan in the hospital, things were different. With Dylan there, *everything* was different. He'd been there five days now, and Ashley had volunteered as a candy striper for three of them—instead of just on Monday. Why not? Two of her club meetings had been cancelled this week so she had extra time to spare.

Ashley knocked again. No way did she want to catch Dylan coming out of the bathroom or changing his clothes or something.

"Yeah?"

"Hi, Dylan. I brought you some mail," Ashley said in her most cheerful candy striper voice. Then she noticed he was shaking a baby's rattle. And on a small table next to his bed were several packages, most of them wrapped in light blue wrapping paper. "Wow. Where did all this come from?"

"Beats me," Dylan said, sounding totally bewildered. "It's a bunch of baby things—addressed to me. Isn't that weird?"

Ashley felt her face coloring. "Some of the kids

at school can be *so* cruel," she told Dylan softly. "I'm sorry."

"What is it? Some kind of a joke? I don't get it," Dylan said. "Look at this junk." He gestured toward the packages with his good arm.

Ashley walked over and looked at the gifts. There was a box of disposable diapers, a baby bottle, and a pacifier.

"Were there any cards?" asked Ashley.

Dylan shrugged. "No."

Brooke, Ashley thought. But she kept her mouth shut.

Ashley noticed a couple more boxes, both unopened, on the window sill. Apparently Dylan didn't want to face what was inside.

"Dylan . . ." Ashley said slowly. "I thought I'd better warn you. Some kids are coming over here today to hang around and see if, well, *anyone else* you know shows up. If you know what I mean."

"No. I don't know what you mean."

Ashley felt exasperated. He was putting on a good show, but she wasn't buying it.

"Look, Dylan, if you want me to, I could find a sign to put on your door. No Visitors—something like that."

"What for?"

"Well, so you wouldn't have to deal with people coming in here and asking you a lot of questions, or making stupid comments."

"What are you talking about? Like, I have something to hide?"

"Well, honestly yes, Dylan. I mean, everyone *knows*."

"Knows *what?*"

Was he really going to pretend like nothing happened? Or like he could go on hiding it forever?

"Everyone knows about . . . well, about your past." Ashley said.

"Oh, great! Like I should be ashamed of my past, or something. Look—I am what I am. Take it or leave it!"

"Fine," Ashley said. "Except maybe you've hurt some people and—"

"Whatever I've done, it's nobody's business but my own. You're acting weird, Ashley, you know that?"

Ashley didn't know what to say. But deep in her heart she was shocked. She never imagined Dylan could be so cold-hearted!

"Okay," she said, dropping his mail on his bed. "Just don't say I didn't warn you!"

CHAPTER 7

COURTNEY WALKED IN through the big glass front doors of the hospital and glanced into the waiting room in the lobby. Brooke and her newest sidekick, Stacy, immediately waved.

What are they doing here? Courtney wondered as she walked toward them.

But then she got the picture. Brooke and Stacy had scoped out the best vantage point to watch everyone who came in the front door. They were planted on a huge gray wool sofa facing the main entrance . . . *waiting for Lisa.*

Every time a young woman walked through

the front door, Brooke stopped talking and looked up. If the woman had a little boy with her, Brooke and Stacy froze.

Was that Lisa? Was *that* Dylan's kid?

"Don't you think Dylan deserves a little privacy?" Courtney said, as she watched Brooke staring at every single woman who came in through the front doors.

"I think this is a public place, and we have every right to sit here," Brooke said. "Besides— don't tell me you wouldn't like to know what Lisa looks like."

Courtney couldn't really deny it—she was just as curious as they were. But she wasn't willing to admit it to Brooke.

"I'm much more concerned about finding my brother," Courtney said truthfully. "I think I'll go see if Dylan's heard from him. Is anyone else up there right now?"

The hospital had a rule limiting visitors to two in the room at a time. Courtney didn't want to get thrown out, but she did want to find out how Dylan was feeling—how he was coping—now that the whole school knew about his secret past.

"Yeah. Chris and Roxanne are up there," Stacy said. "But I don't think they know about

Lisa. They both cut school today."

Chris was a friend of Dylan's, a guy who sometimes played in Dylan's band. He was cool, but Courtney didn't like him much, and she hated Roxanne, the girl Chris hung out with. What was there to like? Roxanne spent all her time sneering at people, putting them down, and slouching around in her "I'm dangerous—look out" black leather jackets.

No—Courtney didn't really want to run into them in Dylan's room. In fact, when they were around, she even wondered why she wanted to get involved with Dylan in the first place.

Still, it was driving her crazy not to see Dylan. She had to find out what he was feeling . . . what was going on up there.

She headed for the elevator and rode to the fourth floor.

Loud music was blaring from behind Dylan's door—so loud that he obviously couldn't hear Courtney knock. She opened the door and went in, but before she could even pull the door closed again, a nurse came in behind her. Chris, Roxanne, and Dylan were laughing and barely noticed either of them until the nurse walked over to the cassette player and pulled the plug.

"Other people are trying to sleep. They are trying to recover from conditions that are quite serious," she said.

"Ooooooh. She's giving you a tongue lashing, Dyl," Chris said, mocking the nurse.

"And another thing," the nurse went on. "The rules say only two visitors in the room at a time. Somebody has to leave."

"How about me?" Dylan cracked.

"Somebody out—now," she said, jerking her head toward the door as she left.

"Yes, sergeant!" Chris yelled after her. His voice echoed down the hall.

Courtney stood off to the side, and Chris and Roxanne temporarily ignored her. But Dylan gave her a private smile when no one else was looking.

"Well, we've got to hit the road anyway," Chris said. "Catch you later."

"Yeah, Dylan. See you when you get out of jail," Roxanne said.

"Later," Dylan said. As soon as they were gone, he turned toward Courtney and said softly, "Hi."

"Hi."

"I'm glad you're here."

"Me, too." She gave him a warm smile, and at the same time noticed that he had put her bouquet of flowers in his water pitcher. Right next to his bed. They didn't look too droopy, either. The roses were on the window sill, farther away.

Courtney's heart beat faster.

"Yeah, like, I was hoping maybe you could help me figure out what's going on. Why people are acting so weird around me."

"Well . . . I guess it's because they're all surprised to find out that you . . . well . . ."

"That I what?"

"Well, that you have a past."

"That's the same stuff Ashley said!" he snapped. "What's wrong with my past?"

"Dylan . . . I don't know how to say this, but, well, everyone knows about Lisa. You can't hide it anymore."

"Who's Lisa?"

"You don't have to pretend with me, Dylan. I *know* who Lisa is. We all do."

"Oh, yeah? Who?"

Okay, Courtney thought. You're going to make me say it.

"The mother of your child. The person who had your son."

There was a long silence while Dylan just stared at her.

"I guess you couldn't keep it a secret forever, Dylan."

"Is everybody crazy?" he said coldly. "I don't have a son."

"Dylan . . . why are you still denying it? I mean, maybe it was a mistake. But you should take some responsibility. It's not anyone else's fault."

"Look—I don't know anyone named Lisa. And I *don't* have a son." He looked at Courtney like he was giving her one more chance—and that was all. "Do you believe me?"

What was Courtney supposed to say? Admit that she'd snooped around in his room? Even though it was Brooke's fault, she didn't think Dylan would forgive her for reading the note.

"I just think it's a waste of energy to pretend he doesn't exist," Courtney said, trying to sound sympathetic and firm at the same time.

"You *don't* believe me!"

Courtney was silent. She wanted to believe him, but she just couldn't.

"Just get out of here," Dylan said. He walked to

the window and stood looking out, his back to her.

"Listen, Dylan, I . . . I just want you to know that, no matter what happened in the past, I'm—you know—on your side."

Silence. Dead silence. Courtney felt herself beginning to cry, but she choked back the tears and said through a strained voice, "Well, I'll see you sometime."

Silence. He was probably never going to speak to her again.

Courtney held her breath, hoping he'd change his mind and tell her to stay. When he didn't, she walked slowly to the door.

"Courtney?"

Please ask me to stay, she thought. Please.

Her heart pounded. "Yes?"

"Has Billy turned up yet?"

"Oh. No, he didn't." Courtney's throat tightened up again, the way it did every time she thought about Billy.

"Well, I've been thinking about something Billy said once. And I wondered—did you try your grandmother's house?"

"Of course. We called her days ago."

"Oh. Well, I just thought maybe he went to hide out in that old barn on her property."

"The barn?"

"Yeah. One time, when my dad was going to kick the band out of our garage, Billy took me there. He said he loved hanging out in the barn. Said maybe we could rehearse the band there. But I guess you already thought of that."

"Dylan, you're wonderful! Thanks!" Courtney said as she flew toward the elevator.

CHAPTER 8

THE SUN WAS slipping toward the horizon when Courtney arrived at her grandmother's farm. She got off the bus, then stood at the side of the road for half a moment, debating whether to go to the house first, or head straight for the barn. She had thought about asking her mother to drive her but she didn't want to get her mom's hopes up. Now Courtney wondered if she should let her grandmother know she was there. The house was set far back from the road, so she knew her grandmother hadn't seen her arrive. The kitchen lights looked like pinpoints in the distant light of early evening.

I'd better get to the barn before the sun goes down, Courtney decided. Otherwise I won't be able to see a thing in the dark. Besides, she thought, there was no sense getting her Grandma's hopes up either. What if Billy wasn't out there?

It was a long walk across the grass to the driveway, and then an even longer walk down the private road to the abandoned barn. No one ever used the barn anymore, except to store things they didn't want but couldn't bring themselves to throw away. Courtney hurried, running the last bit of the way.

What were the chances? she asked herself. If I were Billy, I wouldn't have been able to stay in this barn, in the pitch-black darkness, for even one night.

She pushed open the huge barn door that slid on rusty runners and peered inside.

"Billy?" Courtney called softly at first, almost as if she were afraid to disturb whoever or whatever might be waiting for her.

It took a minute for her eyes to adjust to the dark.

"Billy?"

There was no answer.

Courtney walked inside and stood in the huge

open space for a moment, until she could see fairly well. There was still enough light from the setting sun . . .

Enough to see that Billy wasn't there.

"Billy?" Courtney called desperately. "Billy!"

Nothing. No answer. No sound of movement.

Oh no, Courtney thought. All at once she realized that this was their last hope. And Billy wasn't there.

She turned around and headed back toward the big sliding door.

"Courtney?"

Courtney whirled around and stared into the darkness again. Then suddenly she remembered: the hayloft!

"Billy?"

"Up here."

He *was* there! Thank God, she thought. She heard movement, but couldn't see a thing.

"Where are you, Billy? Come down, please," she called plaintively. "I can't see."

"Come up," he said. His voice sounded so small, like the whimper of an injured animal. It reminded Courtney of when they were younger and he would run to her with a scraped knee.

"Okay. I'm coming up," she said. She dropped her books and bag on the barn floor and climbed the ladder, trying not to step on her long skirt. It took a moment for her eyes to adjust to the dark. When she got to the top, she saw Billy huddled on the far side of a mound of hay.

Billy turned on a small flashlight and set it in the hay, facing up, so that Courtney could find him.

"Hi," he said. He sounded miserable.

"Are you all right?" Courtney held her breath, waiting for the answer.

"Yeah—I guess so."

"Oh, Billy! We were so worried!" Courtney crawled toward him through the hay, letting out a sob. When she reached him, she threw her arms around him and cried. "How could you scare us like this?" she said in a broken voice.

"I'm sorry, Courtney," Billy said, his voice sounding smaller than ever. "But what was I supposed to do? I killed Dylan!"

"No, no, no, you didn't," Courtney said quickly. "Dylan's not dead. He has a broken wrist and maybe some nerve damage." And a lot of personal problems, Courtney thought to herself. "But he's going to be okay."

"Really?" Billy looked like he could hardly believe her. "But I saw him! He was just lying there, not moving!" Billy's voice was filled with the panic and anxiety he'd been holding in for five days. "And it was my fault. I made him race, I really did, Courtney."

"I know what you thought, but you were wrong," Courtney said in a comforting voice. "Dylan's fine. He really is. And you didn't make him race. He did it because he wanted to."

Billy let out a gasp of relief, and Courtney could see the tension draining out of him. His whole body seemed to collapse in the hay, and he trembled, about to cry himself.

"Are you okay?" Courtney asked, wiping her tears away. "Mom and Dad have been worried sick about you. We *all* have. Have you been here the whole time?"

Billy nodded and cleared his throat. "I sneaked into Grandma's house late at night and got some food from her refrigerator." He reached under the hay and pulled out his stash: an apple, some bread, grapes, cookies, and a package of bologna.

Courtney looked at the food, then hugged Billy again, as more tears started running down her face. It was the relief of finding Billy—and the strangeness of knowing Dylan's secret—all pouring out of her at the same time.

"Come on," Courtney said, when she had stopped crying. "We've got to call Mom right away."

They headed toward Grandma's house, and gave her a real start when they appeared at the back door. Then it took about an hour and a half to make all their phone calls, and for Billy to go through his story three times—once for Grandma, once for his mom, and again for his dad. Finally their mother picked them up and drove them both to the hospital so Billy could see Dylan.

Courtney rushed into the hospital lobby, excited to have Billy with her. Even through the revolving doors, she could see Ashley and Kelly, and Brooke and Stacy. Two older guys from school were just leaving the hospital when they saw Billy and Courtney.

"Hey, it's Billy!" one of the guys called out. "He's back!"

Everybody crowded around Billy and he soaked up all the attention, while Courtney just stayed off to the side and smiled.

Then all of a sudden, Courtney became aware that someone was tapping her on the shoulder and trying to squeeze past her. Without meaning to, Courtney and her friends had blocked the main entrance, making it difficult for anyone to come in.

Courtney stepped aside, then turned around and started to apologize to the person behind her. But as soon as she saw who it was, the words "I'm sorry" stuck in her throat.

Behind her stood a girl about 19 or 20 with shoulder-length brown hair, gorgeous blue eyes, and fabulous legs. She was carrying a box of candy in one hand—and pushing a baby stroller with the other! The boy in the stroller was about nine months old, with golden-blond hair and sweet, sad eyes. Just like Dylan's.

Courtney froze and glanced at her friends. No one was paying attention—they were all too busy talking to Billy. When she looked at the girl again, she was standing at the information desk, asking questions.

Courtney edged over and tried to listen. She couldn't catch it all, but she heard the woman say something about, "Are you a family member?" Then she heard a name.

Lisa.

This was it. This was the one! Courtney swung

her head toward her friends, but no one noticed.

Good, Courtney thought. I'd rather follow Lisa alone, anyway. Why not? It would be the perfect ending to a perfectly traumatic week.

Casually hanging back, trying not to be too obvious, Courtney followed Lisa into the elevator. Then a whole crowd of nurses and doctors got in. Courtney had to stand at the very back of the elevator to avoid being squashed.

And she couldn't even get a better look at Dylan's baby.

The elevator stopped on every single floor and Courtney thought she would explode, waiting to finally get out on four. And then what? she asked herself. Follow Lisa into Dylan's room and say to him, "See? I knew you were lying!" And then leave them alone so they could plan their son's college education, or whatever it was they wanted to talk about!

As usual, Courtney got off the elevator on the fourth floor. For a moment she just stood there, but then she heard a voice from behind her saying "Excuse me." The voice was soft and vulnerable-sounding. It was Lisa.

"Oh, sorry," Courtney said, stepping aside.

"That's okay," Lisa said. "I'm not even sure where I'm going."

She looked at the room numbers on the wall, then headed off toward the South Wing.

Wait a minute, Courtney wanted to call. You're going the wrong way. Dylan's room was to the right. Room 443—in the North Wing. But something held her back, so she just kept following Lisa.

Courtney walked down the hall and turned the corner in the South Wing, just in time to see Lisa going into a room.

She'll be out in a sec, Courtney thought, hovering near the door, ready to look casual again and keep moving.

But Lisa didn't come out.

Courtney moved closer—close enough to hear. There was conversation. Lisa and some guy.

"Patrick? Are you awake?"

"Yeah, I'm awake. Well, hi, Lise. You look great, as usual. What a surprise! I never figured *you'd* come."

"Didn't you read the note I sent?"

Was this Dylan's Lisa? Was she in the wrong room or not? Courtney couldn't stand it any longer. She stepped a little closer and peeked through the crack in the door. There were red roses sitting beside the bed.

"What note?"

"The one with the roses. I told you I'd bring your son to see you, Patrick," Lisa said softly. "Brian, this is your daddy. Do you remember Daddy?"

Wait a minute, Courtney thought. Roses . . . one-year-old son . . . do you remember Daddy?

What room was this, anyway?

Courtney looked at the room number and suddenly everything was clear.

CHAPTER 9

COURTNEY RAN DOWN the hall and turned the corner toward Dylan's room in the North Wing. She was so excited, she didn't even bother to knock before going in. Dylan was alone, listening to music on headphones.

"Hi." She mouthed the word since she knew he couldn't hear her.

Dylan gave her a weird look—like he didn't know whether or not to trust her. But finally he took the headphones off and turned off the cassette.

"So? What do *you* want?"

"I have some great news, Dylan," Courtney

said. She was bursting to tell him everything at once. "I found Billy—he was in my grandmother's barn, just like you said! So I wanted to say thank you."

"Hey—that's great!" Dylan sounded relieved. "But why was he hiding out?"

"He thought he was responsible for your accident," Courtney explained softly. "And he thought you were dead."

"Ohhhh." Dylan looked upset. "Poor kid. He must have been really bummed out."

"To say the least. Anyway, I don't think he would have starved to death, but still. Thanks for the idea about the barn. We would have gone crazy if we hadn't found him soon."

"No problem. Your little brother is okay."

"Yeah, he is." Courtney smiled at him. The fact that Dylan liked Billy so much made her love him all the more. "Anyway, Billy wanted to come up here right away," Courtney went on, "but some kids are swarming all over him in the lobby. He's telling everyone all about his great adventure in survival living. But when he comes up, could you tell him that you're not mad at him? About the motorcycle accident, I mean."

"Sure," Dylan said.

Right on cue, Billy walked in the door looking

slightly sheepish. It was obvious that he was still worried about what Dylan thought. Dylan gave him a big smile.

"Hey, Billy, what's happening? I hear *you're* the real rebel these days."

"Hi, Dylan," Billy said shyly.

"So how was it?" Dylan said, still sounding like Billy was his favorite little brother. "Being on your own, I mean?"

"Oh, it was okay. Sort of lonely. There are mice in the barn."

Dylan laughed and then there was a silence. Billy looked like he didn't know what to say. Finally he said, "Listen, Dylan, about the—"

"Forget it," Dylan said. "It wasn't anyone's fault but mine."

"But I mean, are you going to be okay?"

"Yeah," Dylan said, and he actually looked happy for a minute. "I can already move my fingers—" He demonstrated. "And I guess the doctors aren't lying. They did some tests and said there's a good chance I'll be able to play guitar again. But we had to cancel that gig at the Avalon."

"Oh, well," Billy said. "There'll be others. Maybe you can write some new songs while you're on a break from your guitar."

"Yeah, maybe," Dylan agreed. "But I don't think I'll be able to write for a while either. I might have to dictate songs to you."

"Sure. That sounds great!" Billy said. "Hey, Dylan—I only have one question. Are all those kids downstairs waiting to see you? If so, you're sure going to have a lot of visitors!"

Suddenly Dylan wasn't smiling anymore, and Courtney didn't know what to say. She tried to give Billy a look that said "bad subject" but he didn't take the hint. He kept waiting for an answer.

"I'll tell you about that later," Courtney finally said in her most authoritative big sister tone.

"Okay," Billy said, letting it drop. "Anyway, I'm *starved!* I'm going to get something to eat. See you later, Court."

"Hang in there," Dylan called to him. As soon as Billy was gone, Dylan motioned to Courtney with a nod of his head.

"Hey, Courtney," he said. "Come here."

Gladly, she thought. She walked over to where he was standing by the window.

"Give me your hand."

Almost shyly, Courtney held out her hand.

"Watch this," Dylan said. He took her hand

in his—the one with the injured wrist. Then he squeezed it as hard as he could. It almost hurt.

"Ouch," Courtney said, looking at him with surprise.

Dylan smiled. "I've been working on it," he said proudly. "P.T."

"What's P.T.?"

"Physical Therapy. Look how much stronger I am since the first time I tried it."

"Yeah," Courtney said, her voice sounding thin.

Is that what Dylan had been doing the day he held her hand so tightly? Just *physical therapy?*

"What's wrong?" Dylan asked.

"Nothing. I just thought . . ."

"What?"

"Oh, nothing." Courtney took her hand away.

Her lip started to tremble, but just barely. How could she have been such an idiot? Except he was being so sweet right now. Looking at her like he really liked her.

Courtney thought he was about to reach out to her again, when there was a sudden knock at the door.

"Excuse me," a young woman's voice said as she leaned in the door. It was Lisa. And she was holding a vase of red roses. "Sorry to interrupt," she went on, "but I think these flowers are for you. It says Room 443 N on the envelope. They were delivered to Room 443 in the South Wing by mistake."

"That's the other thing I wanted to tell you," Courtney said, rushing to think of a way to explain the whole thing to Dylan. Dylan looked totally confused.

"What?" he asked.

Courtney wasn't sure how to begin. "Those roses you got—they weren't for you." She took the roses from Lisa and set them down near Dylan. Then she gave Lisa the other vase.

"How do you know?" Dylan asked. "There wasn't any card."

But Courtney didn't answer him right away. Instead, she turned to Lisa and said, "There *was* a card, but unfortunately it's missing. Sorry."

"That's okay," Lisa said. "Thanks." She started to leave, then leaned her head back in the door and said, "Hope you feel better" just to be polite.

When she was gone, Dylan said "Are you going to tell me what's going on?"

Slowly, Courtney told Dylan the whole story. About how she and Brooke were in his room, read the card that came with the roses, and got the wrong idea. "It was from that woman who was just here. Lisa."

"Oh, great!" Dylan said, sounding mad.

Courtney pulled out a xerox of the note and showed Dylan what it said.

"Then Brooke spread the news all over school—that you had a son you never saw, and how Lisa was going to bring him to the hospital to see you."

"This is unbelievable," Dylan said.

"I know," Courtney agreed, trying to sound sympathetic instead of guilty.

"So everyone thinks I have a baby? With some girl named Lisa?"

"Yeah, they do right now," Courtney said. "But I'll straighten it out. I'll think of some way to make Brooke spread the *truth* all over the school—although it'll probably kill her to do it."

Dylan laughed. "No, don't bother," he said.

"Are you kidding? Why not?"

"I just think it will be interesting to hang out with this rep for awhile." He laughed a private laugh. "Maybe I'll pass out cigars. Do the proud-new-father thing. It'll be a kick."

"Oh, Dylan," Courtney said. "I really don't think . . ."

But then she stopped. Dylan was Dylan.

There was no way to change him.

And then all of a sudden Courtney looked at the new vase of roses and saw the card, still attached to the vase with a piece of tape. She was bursting to know who the roses were from.

"Well?" she said. "Aren't you going to open the card and find out who those roses are really from?"

"Oh, sure," Dylan said. He pulled the small envelope from the vase, opened it, and took out the card. Slowly, a big smile spread over his face.

"Welllll?" Courtney said again. The suspense was killing her. "Who are they from?" That old girlfriend he told her about? His parents?

Dylan looked up, startled by her voice.

"Oh—What did you say?"

"Come on, Dylan! Who are the roses from?"

Dylan thought about the events of the past few days. The accident . . . his wrist . . . the mix-up with the roses . . . everyone hanging out in the lobby to find out about his personal life. And then he looked over at Courtney.

No way, he thought to himself. He had to keep *something* private.

"That's *my* secret," he said, smiling again and tearing up the card.